Ancient Thunder

Leo Yerxa

Groundwood Books
House of Anansi Press
Toronto   Berkeley

For Max and the critters

WHEN I was a child I much admired the native people of the Great Plains as I watched them ride across the screen in movies. In recent years I've had the pleasure to acquaint myself with a few horses and rekindle my childhood interest. Though my riding lacks the grace and skill of my childhood idols, being in the company of horses is a great joy. These magnificent creatures, combined with the traditional clothing of the native people of the plains, were the inspiration for this book.

The clothing in the illustrations is handmade watercolor paper treated to give it the appearance of leather. But the treatment process destroyed the paper's surface, and painting on it became a nightmare. I experimented with different paints and found that a mix of watercolor and gouache worked best. The patterns for the shirts and dresses are loosely based on designs that I've seen in museums and books over the years.

Leo Yerxa
Ottawa, 2006

The Strawberry Moon (Ode-imini-giizis in Ojibway) is the month of June.

At the rise of the Strawberry Moon

To hooves
of ancient
thunder

In the tall grass, born

To run
with the first
sparkles of
new daylight

Over a sea of grass

Chasing the buffalo

And the
antelope, too

Racing over the tall grass

Resting in the eve

In moonlight, sleeping

Running again
at daybreak

Beating
the earth drum

Carrying man

On hooves of ancient thunder

Groundwood Books / House of Anansi Press
110 Spadina Avenue, Suite 801, Toronto, Ontario M5V 2K4
or c/o Publishers Group West
1700 Fourth Street, Berkeley CA 94710

We acknowledge for their financial support of our publishing
program the Canada Council for the Arts, the Government of Canada
and the Ontario Arts Council.

Canada Council   Conseil des Arts
for the Arts   du Canada

ONTARIO ARTS COUNCIL
CONSEIL DES ARTS DE L'ONTARIO
an Ontario government agency
un organisme du gouvernement de l'Ontario

With the participation of the Government of Canada
Avec la participation du gouvernement du Canada

Library and Archives Canada Cataloguing in Publication
Yerxa, Leo
Ancient thunder / Leo Yerxa.
ISBN 978-1-55498-127-4
1. Wild horses — Juvenile literature. 2. Picture books for children.
I. Title.
SF360.Y47 2012   j599.665'5   C2011-904537-0

The illustrations are in dyes on handmade and processed paper.
Design by Michael Solomon
Printed and bound in Malaysia